Text copyright © 2013 by Shirley Hughes
Illustrations copyright © 2013 by Clara Vulliamy

First U.S. edition 2014

Library of Congress Catalog Card Number 2013955663
ISBN 978-0-7636-7369-7

LEO 19 18 17 16 15 14
10 9 8 7 6 5 4 3 2 1

Printed in Heshan, Guangdong, China

This book was typeset in Bodoni Antiqua.
The illustrations were done in pencil, ink, and digital collage.

Candlewick Press
99 Dover Street
Somerville, Massachusetts 02144

visit us at www.candlewick.com

DIGBY O'DAY

In the Fast Lane

Shirley Hughes

illustrated by

Clara Vulliamy

CANDLEWICK PRESS

Contents

And some fun extras at the back!

Digby O'Day is always ready for adventure, and he never says no to a challenge. He's the free-wheeling, car-racing hero of our story, so we caught up with him at home to see if he would answer a few questions for us. . . .

Hello, Digby! First, an easy question. What is your favorite color?

Hello. Favorite color? That would be red, like my car.

And what's your favorite biscuit?

I like a custard cream, but Percy prefers a Jammie Dodger.

What is your most precious possession?

My car!

Oh, of course! Can you describe your perfect day out for us?

A day out motoring with my friend Percy. We'd pack a picnic and head for the seaside.

Sounds lovely! What is your most extravagant purchase?

Once I bought fifty-four bow ties! They were on sale, though.

And now tell us about your ideal evening.

Well, I think it would have to be sitting by the fire with Percy. We'd be watching a cooking show on television, and we'd have our supper on a tray.

What's your most embarrassing moment?

Oh, dear, I'm not sure I want to tell you. Well, if I must, it would be the time my next-door neighbor Lou Ella saw me doing my morning exercises in my underpants.

Whoops! And finally, tell us a joke.

What do you get if you cross a dog and a daisy? A cauliflower! (A collie-flower—get it?)

Ha! Wonderful—thank you, Digby, for telling us a bit about yourself, and about your friend Percy, too!

Lou Ella
Likes:
pink
fast cars
ice-cream sundaes

The friendly family
Likes:
holidays
sweets
giving a helping hand

Ron Barrakan
Owns the petrol station
and diner
Don's brother

Don Barrakan
Owns the car-repair shop
Ron's brother

Auntie Dot
Busy with her
tomato plants
Friendly Dad's aunt

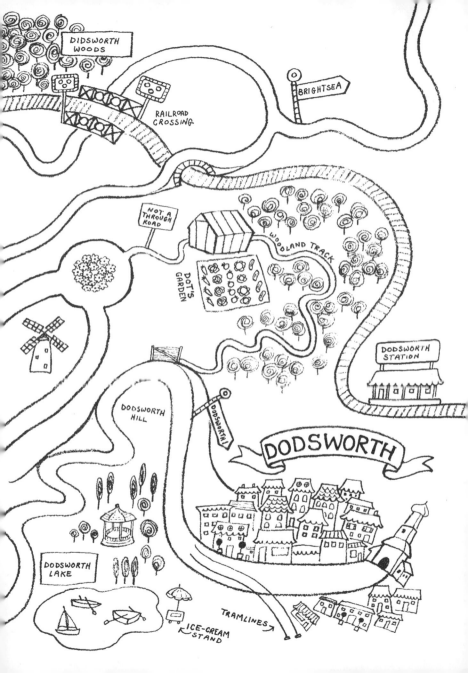

Chapter One

Digby O'Day loved his car and took
great care of it. The car was not new,
but it was a very clean machine.
His friend Percy often came over
to help him polish the bodywork
until it shone.

Digby's neighbor Lou Ella bought a new car every year, always a very expensive one. It annoyed Digby a lot when she drove past his house and tooted her horn.

Toot!
Toot!

Digby often took Percy for a day in
the country. Digby drove, and Percy
admired the view.

One day they took a road that led
up a steep hill with hairpin bends.
Halfway up, the car started to
make funny noises.

Thwonk!

Clunk!

Splutter!

7

Just then, who should drive past
them but Lou Ella, in her brand-new
pink convertible.

She pulled up a little way
ahead and called out,

"You seem to be in trouble! Sorry
I can't help. It's just that I know
nothing about engines—silly old me!"
Then she waved and drove on.

Black smoke was now coming out of the back of Digby's car. Then it began to slide slowly backward.

Digby put on the brake, but the car wouldn't stop.

"We're going the wrong way!" said Percy.

"Yes, I can see that," replied Digby rather crossly. He was busy trying to steer backward. The car slid faster and faster, then spun around, and they found themselves facing down the hill.

The car sped on, reaching a bend
where there was a steep cliff. They
careened off the road, broke through
the railing, and went right to
the edge, where . . .

Oh, phew!

the car stopped.

They were halfway over a sheer drop. Percy looked down, then covered his eyes.

"We'd better get out," said Digby. But when they tried to move, the car wobbled.

"It might help if you could climb over into the backseat, Percy," said Digby.

Percy did, but he wasn't heavy enough to make much difference.

Digby didn't dare get out of the car to push it back onto the road, because every time he tried to open the door, the car slipped a little farther over the edge.

They both sat there for a long time.
"I'm hungry," said Percy. "I wish
we'd brought a picnic."

Digby was hungry, too, but he tried
to be brave.

At last a car came around the bend
and stopped.

It was a friendly family—Mum,
Dad, and three little ones in the back.

Dad hopped out at once to help. He tied a rope to the back of Digby's car, and the whole family heaved and lugged until slowly, slowly, they managed to pull it back onto the road.

All the little ones cheered.

"You are a true gentleman," said Digby, shaking Dad's hand as they said good-bye.

It was a long walk home.

Lou Ella was standing at her gate as they trudged up the road.

"Oh, dear, have you had a breakdown?" she said. "It's really time you got a new car, Digby."

Digby didn't answer. He and Percy just walked into the house and closed the door.

Chapter Two

One day soon afterward, a very
exciting notice appeared in town:

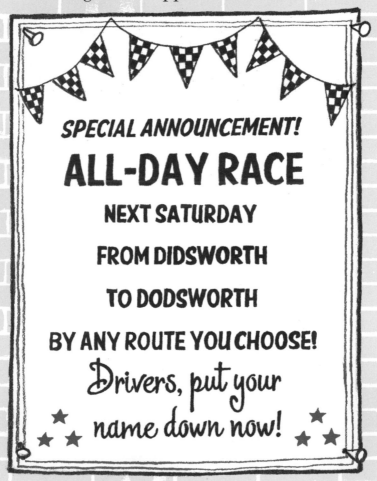

SPECIAL ANNOUNCEMENT!

ALL-DAY RACE

NEXT SATURDAY

FROM DIDSWORTH

TO DODSWORTH

BY ANY ROUTE YOU CHOOSE!

Drivers, put your
name down now!

"How lucky that my car has been fixed!" said Digby. "It's as good as new—well, almost—so I can join the race!"

"Can I be your co-driver?" asked Percy.

"Certainly, Percy. But I will do the driving."

When the big day came, lots of cars were lined up at the start. Lou Ella was there, wearing a specially designed motoring hat.

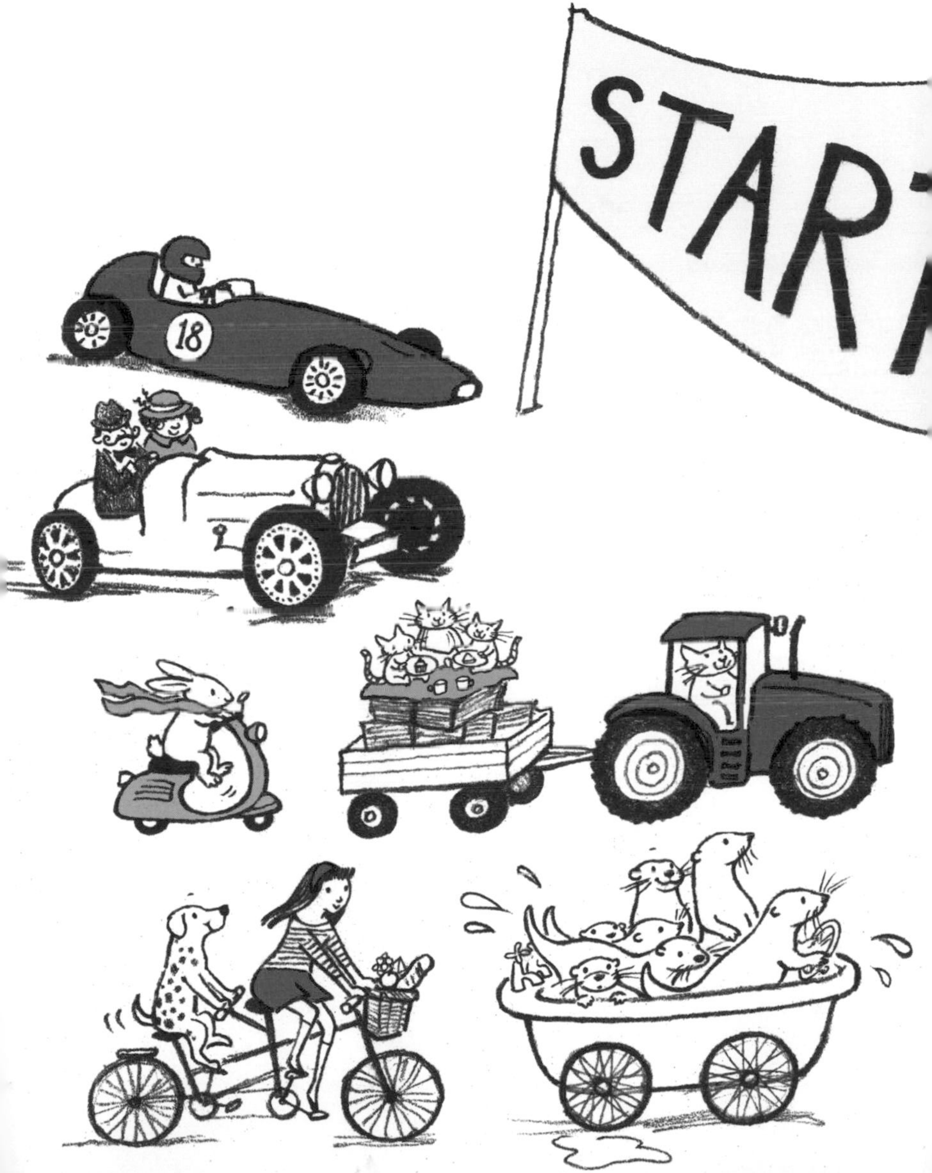
18

When the starting flag went down, she zoomed off ahead of everyone in a cloud of dust.

Digby's car chugged along nicely.
Percy read the map.

Sometimes other drivers passed
them . . .

and tooted their horns.

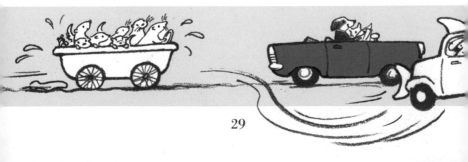

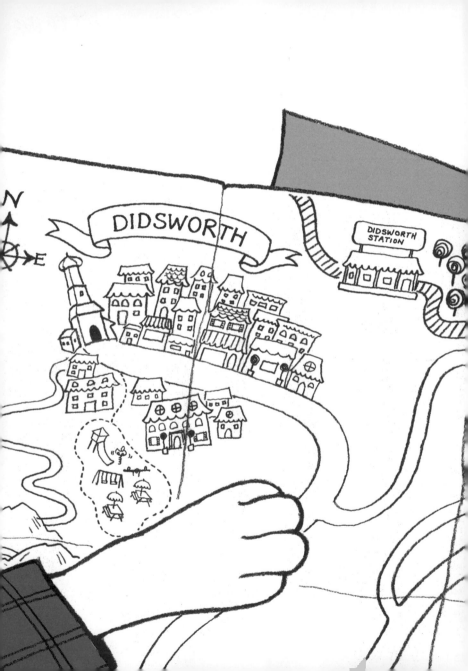

"Do you think you could drive a bit faster, Digby?" said Percy after a while.

"This is as fast as she'll go," answered Digby.

More and more cars seemed to be passing them.

"Let's try this side road," said Percy, pointing to the map. "It looks like a shortcut."

They turned off and tootled along happily.

"This is more like it," said Digby. "I'm sure we're making good time now."

Just then they came to a railroad crossing. The warning light was telling them to STOP!

The gates were beginning to close. Digby drove faster.

They were halfway across when the car suddenly stalled. Then it stopped. The wheels churned around and around. They were stuck on the railroad track!

The gates were nearly closed. They could hear the train coming around the bend.

Digby jammed his foot down hard
on the accelerator.

The car gave a great jolt and shot a few feet backward. Then it shot forward. They scraped through just as the gates clanged shut behind them.

Digby pulled up. They sat there, breathless, listening to the train roar past.

"Perhaps this shortcut isn't such a good idea after all," said Percy.

Chapter Three

Meanwhile, Lou Ella was
zipping along ahead of everyone
else. She was doing so well that
when she saw a sign that read:

she thought she would stop and treat
herself to a good lunch.

Ron Barrakan was standing by the petrol pumps as she drew up.

"Fill up my tank and give the car a thorough clean," she said, tossing him her car keys. "I am well ahead in the Big Didsworth to Dodsworth Race, and I want the car to look good when I come in first!"

"Certainly, madam," Ron replied. But there was a problem, because Ron wasn't just the petrol-station attendant. He was also the car-wash attendant, chef, and waiter all rolled into one.

He ran around to the back of the diner and changed into a spotless white apron to take her order.

Lou Ella was too busy studying the menu to notice that the waiter was the same person.

Ron arranged the food carefully
on the plate and set it before her with
a flourish. Then he sprinted back
to wash and polish her car. Halfway
through, he had to break off and run
back to serve her dessert.

He only just had time to give the car a final wipe when he heard her calling impatiently for her bill.

"This is far too expensive!" she said when she saw it. "The food here is horrible, and the service was far too slow!"

Then she flung down only half
the money, jumped into her car, and
drove off, leaving no tip.

Ron was annoyed because he had done his best. He rang up his brother, Don, who lived farther up the road, and told him all about it. Don was even more annoyed.

Don had a car-repair shop. Over the door it said:

DON BARRAKAN
EXHAUSTS
AND
TIRES

Nearby was a signpost that pointed the way to Dodsworth. Don was so irritated that he went straight out and turned the sign in the opposite direction.

DIDSWORTH 7

CAMPSITE 18

DODSWORTH 11

Minutes later, Lou Ella swept past and zoomed off, going the wrong way. Then Don turned the sign back again, smiling triumphantly.

Chapter Four

Digby and Percy were now back on the main road.

"I'm afraid we've lost a bit of time," said Digby. Cars of all sizes were speeding along, some passing others recklessly. Digby drove carefully, as always. He noticed a car that had broken down at the side of the road.

ice cream · drinks

18

DIGBY O'DAY

Steam was coming out of the open
hood. None of the drivers would stop
to help.

Digby pulled over at once.
"In trouble?" he asked.

The car owner turned out to be none other than the driver who had helped them when they were stuck on the cliff edge. Now Mum was upset and the three little ones were crying in the back.

"We're not even in the race. We're just trying to get home," said Dad gloomily.

"Don't worry—it's *our* turn to help *you*!" answered Digby.

Together they tied a rope to each
car while Percy found some sweets
for the children.

"How can I thank you?" said Dad after Digby had towed them to Don Barrakan's car-repair shop. "I'm afraid we've ruined your chances in the race. But if you turn left at the next roundabout and then follow the sign that says:

NOT A
THROUGH
ROAD

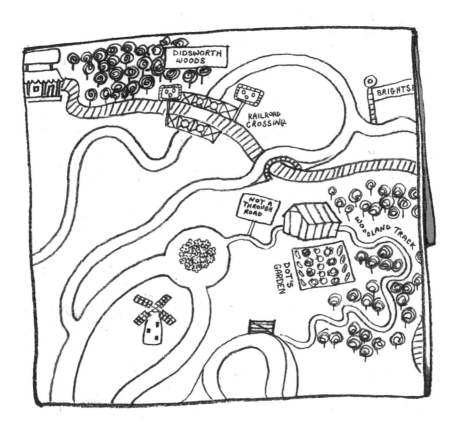

you will come to my auntie Dot's
garden, and she may be able to
help you."

Percy was doubtful as they drove off, but Digby said, "Why not? We've got nothing to lose now!"

Chapter Five

Meanwhile Lou Ella had gone a long way down the wrong road before she realized her mistake. She screeched to a halt, made a dangerous U-turn, and began to speed back. She had not gone far before she ran smack into the back of a big farm truck full of sheep.

The back doors flew open, and the
sheep came out, *baa*-ing joyously.

They spread in different directions
all over the road.

Lou Ella tooted her horn
impatiently.

"Get those silly creatures out of the way, can't you?" she shouted at the farmer.

"It's your fault!" he shouted back. "You were going too fast!"

Lou Ella's car was surrounded. There was nothing she could do.

In the Fast Lane

It took the farmer

a very

long time

to get all the sheep

back into the truck.

By this time Digby and Percy had found the NOT A THROUGH ROAD sign and bumped up the dirt track. Dot was watering her tomato plants.

"Friends of my nephew? Of course I'll help you," she said. "There's a narrow road at the back of my greenhouse that leads through the woods and comes out on the main road right at the top of Dodsworth Hill. You'll be there in no time!"

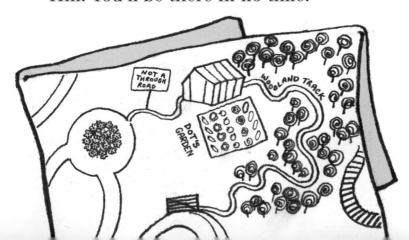

It was a very bumpy road,
and when they got into the woods,
Digby had to swerve in and out of
the trees.

The car leaped and bounced.

"I hope I'm not going to be sick!" said Percy.

"No time for *that*," said Digby firmly.

At last they came to a gate at the top of the hill and Digby jumped out to open it.

Below them lay the little town of
Dodsworth. There was no other car
in sight.

"I do believe we're in the lead!" Digby shouted as he jumped back in the car.

Chapter Six

But at that moment, the engine
suddenly stalled. It made a spluttering
noise.

Then it stopped.

Digby tried and tried to start it
again. Nothing happened.

He got out, opened the hood, and looked inside.

Valuable minutes were ticking away.

"I'll have to give her a push. You
sit in the driver's seat and steer,
Percy."

Digby strained and pushed. The
car edged forward, but still the engine
would not start. Then they heard
another car coming up behind them.
It was Lou Ella!

As she drew level with them, she
slowed down and called out, "Spot of
bother? I told you to buy a new car,
Digby. See you both in Dodsworth
after I've won!"

Then she laughed shrilly and
sped on.

At that moment, Digby's car began
to move forward more quickly. The
engine hadn't started, but it was
going downhill on its own, gathering
speed as it went. Digby only just had
time to jump in and take over the
steering wheel.

They were going faster now, but
Lou Ella was still ahead. As they came
near to Dodsworth, cheering crowds
lined the route.

"Come on, Digby!" they shouted. "You can do it!"

Chapter Seven

Dodsworth was an old town that used to have trams long ago. The tramlines were still there in the road.

Now, suddenly, Lou Ella found that the wheels of her car had somehow gotten stuck in the iron tracks.

"Lucky for me they're going in the right direction!" she muttered as she jammed her foot on the accelerator.

In her rearview mirror, she could
see Digby's car close behind her.

The main square was in sight.
Digby could see the checkered flag.

At that moment, the engine of
Digby's car suddenly spluttered into life.

"*She's going!*" cried Digby.

"Come on, come on!"

squeaked Percy.

Other cars were coming up
behind Lou Ella now. She was only
a short distance from the finish when,
to her horror, she realized that the
tramlines were branching off away
from the route.

She found her car being carried not toward victory but onto a side street!

She tried to reverse, but it was too
late. She could hear wild cheers from
the crowd as Digby and Percy passed
the finish line.

"What a day! What a race!"
said Digby to Percy that
evening as they sat together
admiring their splendid trophy.
There was a special certificate, too,
signed by the mayor of Dodsworth.

After the presentation, Digby and Percy had been carried shoulder-high by the cheering crowd.

See page 5 for more photos

The DODSWORTH DAILY

DIGBY O'DAY IS WINNER!

The Didsworth to Dodsworth Race came to a nail-biting finish today when everyone's favorites— Digby O'Day and his co-driver, Percy— won by a whisker!

"DELIGHTED!" said Digby.

...r of Dodsworth

ADVERTISEMENT
Dodsworth Delights Café
BREAKFAST
LUNCH
TEA

FINISH

"It took them a really long time
to get Lou Ella's car out of the
tramlines, didn't it?" said Percy.

"Will you get a new car now, Digby?" asked Percy the next morning.

"Oh, no, I don't think so. Let's give her a good clean and take her on an outing."

As they were loading their picnic into the trunk, they saw Lou Ella standing at her gate. She was still wearing her motoring hat and trying to look as if nothing had happened.

"Sorry you had a spot of bother," called Digby. "Better luck next time. Perhaps you'd better buy a new car?"

Lou Ella did not reply.

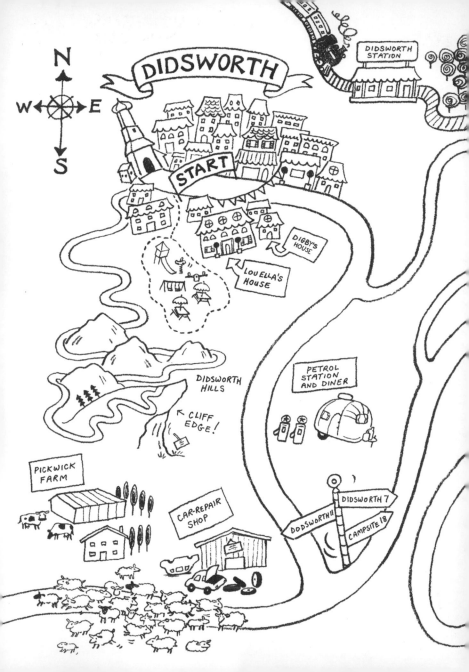

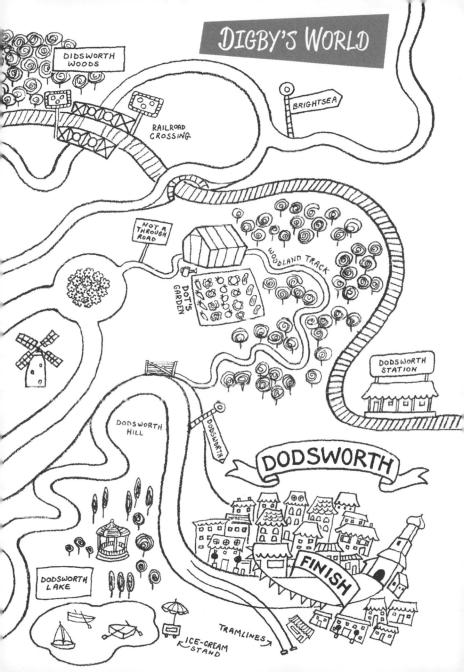

I SPY

Look out of the window (or around the car) and pick something you can see (for example, a sheep). Then say, "I spy, with my little eye, something beginning with *s*" (or whichever is the first letter of the word you have picked). The other people in the car have to guess what you are thinking of: sand, sun, sweets, or sandwiches!

The License Plate Game

Pick a license plate and look at the letters in it. Can you make a word from them? For example, a license plate with BCK in it might make the word BACK or BUCKLE or BUCKET!

WHO AM I?

Think of an object, animal, plant, or person. The other people in the car have to guess who or what you are by asking you questions that can only be answered with "Yes" or "No." For example, "Are you female?" "Would I find you at the beach?" "Are you larger than this car?" "Do you like custard creams?"

Tell jokes and sing songs!

Digby and Percy know lots of (terrible) jokes, which they like to tell on car trips. Here's one of their favorites: **What do you call a country where everyone has to drive a pink car? *A pink car nation.*** Try telling jokes with your family! Percy also likes to sing songs in the car, though Digby isn't quite so enthusiastic. What's your favorite song to sing?

I'M GOING TO . . .

This is a memory game. One person picks somewhere for you all to go (for example, to a museum), and starts the game off by picking an object they are taking with them: "I'm going to a museum, and I'm bringing my glasses." The next person repeats this and adds something of their own: "I'm going to a museum, and I'm bringing my glasses and my sketchpad." Keep going, and see how many things you can remember (in the right order, of course)!

The Story Game

Make up a story together! One person starts (perhaps with "Once upon a time . . .") and then passes the story to the next person. Let your imaginations run wild! You can use what you see out of the window for inspiration.

Percy's Perfect Car Games

Digby and Percy love going for long car rides. They pack a picnic and set off. Sometimes they follow a map, but sometimes they just like to see where they end up. Percy loves playing games when Digby is driving. Above are some of his favorites.

Crazy Cars!

Can you draw your own wonderful vehicle? Maybe it isn't a car—maybe it's a bathtub with wheels or something else entirely.

Does it fly, or go in water? How many people will fit inside, and what color will it be?

Get some paper and drawing materials, and come up with your own crazy car.

The Digby O'Day Quiz

Digby has written a special quiz to test you! How much can you remember about Digby O'Day in the Fast Lane?

1. What does Digby's license plate say?

2. How often does Lou Ella buy a new car?

3. How many children are there in the friendly family?

4. Where does the all-day race start from?

5. What color is Lou Ella's new car?

6. Who owns the petrol station and diner?

7. What is his brother's name?

8. What kind of farm animal does Lou Ella get surrounded by?

9. What kind of plants is Dot watering?

10. Who wins the all-day race?

11. Who do you think comes in second?

12. What is the name of the newspaper that features Digby and Percy on the front page?

My great-grandfather
Admiral Dexter Duckworth O'Day

Aunt Daisy

Mum and Dad

Me when I was two

My first go-kart

Can you spot Percy and me in our old school photograph?

And finally, introducing Shirley Hughes and Clara Vulliamy — the dashing duo behind Digby and Percy's adventures!

Shirley Hughes

LIKES:
sketchbooks, friendly neighbors, ballroom dancing

DISLIKES:
airports, spiders, waiting in line

Clara Vulliamy

LIKES:
chocolate buttons, goats, motorcycles with sidecars

DISLIKES:
peas, alarm clocks, losing her glasses

And guess what? Clara is Shirley's
daughter! And this is the first book
they have created together!

If you enjoyed

DIGBY O'DAY

In the Fast Lane,

then you'll love Digby and Percy's
next adventure,

DIGBY O'DAY

and the

Great Diamond Robbery

Here's the first chapter. . . .

DiGBY O'DAY

and the Great Diamond Robbery

Chapter One

One fine summer morning, Digby O'Day said to his friend Percy, "I've decided that it's time to take a little vacation. Would you join me, Percy?"

"You bet!" said Percy. "Shall we take the tent and go camping?"

"No, I'm thinking of something a bit more luxurious. I'm booking us in at the Hotel Splendide at Brightsea!"

"The Hotel Splendide! That's one of the fanciest hotels on the coast! Won't it be terribly expensive?"

"Never mind that," Digby replied nonchalantly. "I've been saving up for a long time, and now we deserve a bit of a treat."

"I'd better pack my bow tie," Percy said.

"Oh, yes," said Digby. "And of course we will have to take our dinner jackets to change into in the evening."

"Oh, dear!" said Percy. "I only have the one that belonged to my uncle Gus! I'm afraid it's a bit moth-eaten and has a couple of gravy stains. . . ."

"Never mind. Give it a bit of a wash, Percy, and you'll look fine. Don't forget, you're one of the best ballroom dancers I know—why, you've even won competitions!"

"I'll do my best not to let you down," said Percy bravely.

They both set to work to give Digby's car a good clean, polishing the bodywork until it shone.

It wasn't long before they were driving happily toward Brightsea. They had chosen a quiet side road that had more scenic views than the main road and very little traffic.

They were cruising merrily along when suddenly another car zoomed up behind them, seemingly out of nowhere. It followed closely, almost touching their back bumper, then pulled out and shot past them with inches to spare. There might have been a disastrous crash if Percy hadn't reacted instantly by grabbing the steering wheel.

Digby's car shot up a bank at the side of the road and came to a jolting stop, narrowly missing the fence. The other car was already roaring away into the distance.

They sat for a while, stunned with shock.

"That was a narrow escape!" muttered Digby at last.

"Road hogs!" shouted Percy furiously. "Did you see their license plate?"

"No, unfortunately. I was too busy trying to get out of their way. All I saw was a driver and one passenger. They both had scarves pulled up so you couldn't see their faces properly."

"No good trying to report them for dangerous driving, then," said Percy. "They should be fined or sent to prison. It's a *disgrace*!"

They continued on their journey at a careful pace, feeling very upset.

Adventure and excitement await Digby and Percy when they arrive at the Hotel Splendide. Percy's favorite pop star, the glamorous Peaches Miaow, is staying there, but disaster strikes when her diamond necklace is stolen. Will Digby be able to solve this dastardly crime?

Find out in

DIGBY O'DAY

and the Great Diamond Robbery